W9-BUB-317

Dear Parent:
Your child's love of reading starts here!

Every child learns to read in a different way and at his or her own speed. Some go back and forth between reading levels and read favorite books again and again. Others read through each level in order. You can help your young reader improve and become more confident by encouraging his or her own interests and abilities. From books your child reads with you to the first books he or she reads alone, there are I Can Read Books for every stage of reading:

SHARED READING
Basic language, word repetition, and whimsical illustrations, ideal for sharing with your emergent reader

BEGINNING READING
Short sentences, familiar words, and simple concepts for children eager to read on their own

READING WITH HELP
Engaging stories, longer sentences, and language play for developing readers

READING ALONE
Complex plots, challenging vocabulary, and high-interest topics for the independent reader

ADVANCED READING
Short paragraphs, chapters, and exciting themes for the perfect bridge to chapter books

I Can Read Books have introduced children to the joy of reading since 1957. Featuring award-winning authors and illustrators and a fabulous cast of beloved characters, I Can Read Books set the standard for beginning readers.

A lifetime of discovery begins with the magical words **"I Can Read!"**

Visit www.icanread.com for information on enriching your child's reading experience.

 For information address HarperCollins Children's Books, a division of HarperCollins Publishers, 10 East 53rd Street, New York, NY 10022.
www.icanread.com

Library of Congress catalog card number: 2010936336
ISBN 978-0-06-198940-7 (trade bdg.)—ISBN 978-0-06-198939-1 (pbk.)

11 12 13 14 15 SCP 10 9 8 7 6 5 4 3 2 1 ❖ First Edition

MESSY DOG

BASED ON THE BESTSELLING BOOKS BY JOHN GROGAN

COVER ART BY RICHARD COWDREY

TEXT BY SUSAN HILL

INTERIOR ILLUSTRATIONS BY LYDIA HALVERSON

HARPER

An Imprint of HarperCollins*Publishers*

Mommy was painting the walls of Cassie's room.

Mommy looked at the new paint
and smiled.
"Cassie is going to love this,"
she said.

Rrrrring!

Mommy went to answer the phone.

Mommy had put Marley in the garage
so he wouldn't get into trouble.
But Marley was good at opening doors.

Marley poked his head
into Cassie's room.
Then he poked his head
into the paint can.

“I can help,” Marley thought.
He dipped his tail into the paint.

Then Marley wagged his tail.
“Good job!” Marley thought.
“Cassie is going to love this!”

Uh-oh!

Marley tipped over the paint can.

Paint spilled all over.

“No problem,” thought Marley.

“I’ll just cover it up.”

But even Marley could see

his fix didn’t work.

Marley heard Mommy's footsteps.

He ran and hid in the tub.

“I can finish painting now,”

said Mommy.

“I can’t wait to show Cassie.”

Mommy stopped in her tracks.
“Oh, no!” she yelled.
“This mess has Marley
written all over it!”

Mommy followed Marley's tracks down the hall.

"Marley!" she yelled.

The tracks went into the bathroom.
So did Mommy.
"I know you're in there, Marley!"
she shouted.

Mommy looked in the tub.

Marley was not there.

Mommy was mad!

"You can run, Marley," she yelled,

"but you can't hide!"

Marley could hear Mommy yelling.
He jumped into a pile of leaves
and hid.

“Get that messy dog!”

Mommy yelled.

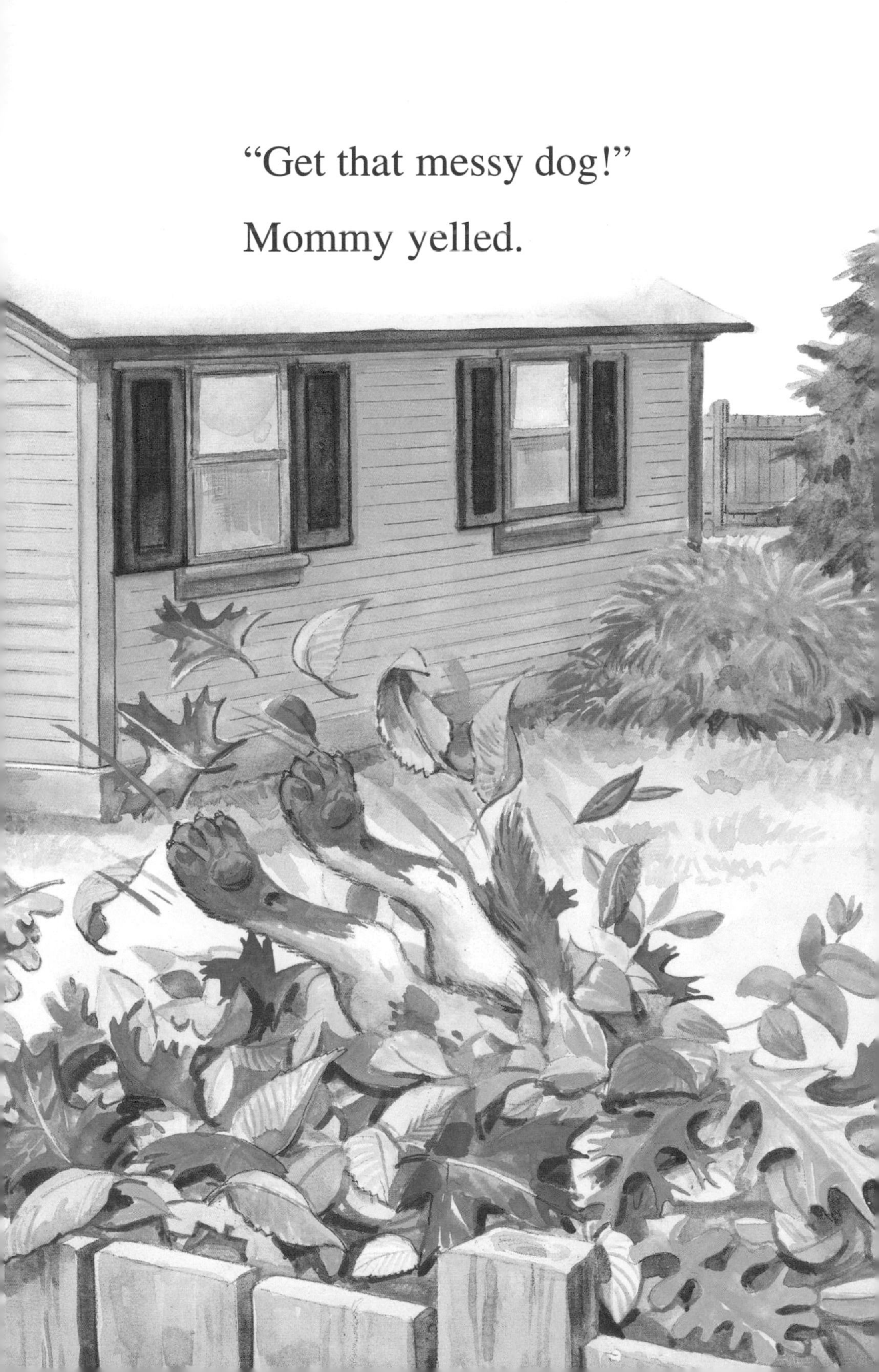

Daddy poked at the leaf pile.

"Any purple dogs in there?"

The leaf pile suddenly exploded!

"Stop, Marley!" Cassie yelled.

But Marley didn't stop.

He ran and tried to hide in a puddle.

“You are one messy dog, Marley,”

Daddy said.

“Let’s clean him up,”

said Mommy.

"Oh, MESSY DOG, Marley!"

said Cassie.

They all went to look
at Cassie's room.
"Don't worry, Cassie," said Mommy.
"I'll paint it again,
with no help from Marley."

"I love it just the way it is!"

Cassie said.

"I knew she would," thought Marley.

"Ruff-ruff!"